T0067875

# His Love Captivated Me

## Cali Redbone

authorHOUSE

*AuthorHouse™*
*1663 Liberty Drive*
*Bloomington, IN 47403*
*www.authorhouse.com*
*Phone: 833-262-8899*

*Published by AuthorHouse   01/19/2023*

*ISBN: 978-1-7283-7781-0 (sc)*
*ISBN: 978-1-7283-7780-3 (e)*

*Library of Congress Control Number: 2023901062*

*Print information available on the last page.*

*Any people depicted in stock imagery provided by Getty Images are models, and such images are being used for illustrative purposes only. Certain stock imagery © Getty Images.*

*This book is printed on acid-free paper.*

After spending time with Raw! It was like a dream come true. A Fairytale. A much needed Vacation. He was everything I hoped and Dreamed of in a man. After the Spa date with my Family I realized how Blessed I was. Why me?? Big Mama from New Orleans, choose me Cali Redbone sweet little thang from California. I can hear telling me "you're going to make a man happy one day baby" "10 years later reminiscing on our conversation . I made it!. When life threw me Lemons You know what your girl did? yes!! Bitch I made Lemonade. Waiting for Raw and Daddy to get in from their fishing trip, All the ladies got in from the Spa tired. We all decided to rest til dinner. "Cali im so tired. He cracked my neck, my back, even my ass bone" "lol. your ass crazy Honey". "I'm serious I was so teansed. I aint got laid in a minute. I'm going to take a nap."

"Dont be in there jacking off lol.

"Hush child, don't be talking like that."

"Forgive me Mama, you look exhausted"

"Girl dont try to change the subject, you need your mouth washed out with soap" as Honey giggles and makes faces at me behind Mama's back. I ask

"Mama you want to lay down?" Yes baby, I feel so relaxed. I needed that massage. baby I love you!"

"I love you more Mama, thank you for all that you do for us, I would not have made it this far."

"Well baby God knew what you needed to settle down and spend time with Family and start your own Family. Raw is the man! made just for you so appreciate your gift. The women down here, lost out on a good man. Cali he loves you, I can tell the way he looks at you. you make his Liver Quiver! ain't that what you say? "awww mama, you so funny"

"Cali I heard him tell your Daddy, Pops I never knew, Love like this. Your daddy likes him for you. Remeber you have Favor with God never forget that!!. You Ms. Cali, you're a special child. You got a Praying man, who loves the Lord. your mama would be so happy for you! I don't know why, she always said you needed a Countryman who will provide for you and love you like no other. You have so many gifts, you need to ask God for guidance in every step you make and take. I don't know why! we are having this conversation baby, only God knows you've come a long way and don't worry about that D.A I'll take care of him with my ice pick."

"Mama don't talk like that,"

"well i'll feed him rat poison"

"Mama you are crazy."

"I'm going to rest, take care of Raw, he is one in a million!. I'm so proud of you and I'm so glad you took my advice!"

"Let me help you."

"No it's ok I got it!

"Mrs. Laura can you please order some food for dinner? There will be no cooking, it's a kick back day. I'm going upstairs to rest. Dinner will be at 8." "What would you like?"

"Whatever you order will be fine."

Walking up the stairs feeling so relaxed entering the room ready to climb in the bed, I get a text from Princess. Saying Cali they found Monalisa, someone beat her half to death.

"I'm on my way to the Hospital, I know you're In New Orleans. Honey not answering her phone" texting her back.

"She's here with me, please dont call Honey, I'll let her know, she will be ready to roll! Madamn Star is here too, When you get there let me know how she is doing. Text me dont want to upset Mama. Omg I knew something might happen to her I felt it.'Lord Touch her, spare her life, save her thinking to myself' like I said before he will pay!! that Dirty Red piss colored nigga!! I'll get his ass myself! This is personal. He hurt my sister. She's a baby just trying to live life without struggling. Trying to get her bag up to help her mom and siblings. Tears rolled down my face thinking it's time to go back to Cali. I must keep it 100% with Raw. I got to tell him. Laying down to rest. Chaney calls me out of the blue. "Hey what's going on Cali? I was thinking about you hard! So I called you!

"I'm in New Orleans, something happened to one of my little sisters. I need you to do something for me "anything for you Cali!"

"Ok i'll be back in a few days i'll call you when I get back"

"ok you good"

"Yes, but, no, are you good?"

"Yes, I'm trying to get my driving licences, so I can get a job."

"Chaney, I got a job and a car for you, you already know this! Me and Chaney go way back. When we were teenagers we did everything together. Me and her, Smokey Loc, Big Darlene, My

3

Sister for life! Laying here thinking, I should have found Monalisa before I left. feeling some type of way a knock at the door.

"Come in" it's Mrs Laura

"Cali I ordered food, got some wine chilling, everything is fine. Is there Something wrong Cali your demeanor, you look like something bothering you?"

"No just tired."

"Ok baby you can talk to me about anything I'm here for you", "thank you". "Ok i'll see you at dinner". "Hey Mrs Laura, you dont work in the kitchen, you run it !!! I dont want you working hard any more!! Oh wait, here's something for you, remember I said I want to pay your house off. And I don't want to hear, no Cali. I'm leaving Wednesday. I would like you to travel with me smiling, I'll see you at seven." "Thank you so much Cali". "No thank you Mrs Laura" . "As she walks out the door I hear her say hallelujah Thank you Jesus for always blessing me". "It's 5:40. I'll rest for a minute. Then get up and run Raw some bath water. Looking at my beautiful Blue Roses I'll put petals down for my King to walk on. As I lay here dozing off Raw texts me" wife i'll be home in an hour. I miss you so much you're going to get this A1 pipe when I get in" smiling! "Pops catching all the damn fish. Crappies and Perch. And a guy here is filet, them" "Ok, babe Love you. Dinner will be ready and your bath you probably smelling like fish, love you. Laying here thinking about Mona praying she is ok." Phone rings, it's Jeveontay. "Hey Cali, it's JV! You heard what happened"? "No, what's going on? Jewels hit Monalisa in the back of her head with a wine bottle. Dirty Red told Jewel Mona is his new bottom Bitch "hell naw" "yes!!! but, you didnt hear it from me. I heard they were having a threesome. It must have gotten good for him, but check this out Dirty Red knocked Jewel front teeth out. Mona got 20 stitches in the back of her head. Dirty

Red went to jail. Big Papa bailed him out", "you mean Big Frank "
no, "Papa from the 9th Ward Black Jeff folks' '. "Oh ok, how's your
dad? "He is doing well". "Is Mona ok ? Yes She's alive," what a relief
I still got to get her. Ok Jv thank you for keeping me updated. I got
you when I get back. Tell Your daddy, ima have some work for you
guys. Now I got to figure out what we are going to do with Madam
stables. I could call big Rella. She got a couple of her son Ricks girls
she could help out. Just thinking out loud. Now I can rest, setting
my alarm clock for 1 hour. Laying here resting my eyes. 1 hour later,
I jumped up to the sound of my alarm buzzing pushing snooze. As
i got up, I grabbed my Roses, pulling them apart, spreading them
on the floor leading to the tub. Running his water, putting in some
Olive Oil, and Eucalyptus, Blue Rose Petals floating in his water.
Lighting some candles. Getting him something to slip on, he really
doesn't need anything to put on, this man God gave me. Smh smiling
with pleasure. Alexa play Deliver me. Music comes on throwing my
hands up Lord you hold the Blueprint to my Life. I can hear them
pulling in the garage, looking out the window. it's such a beautiful
night, wind blowing the sun setting. Texting Mrs Laura can you
please make sure Maria puts fresh towels in Daddy's bathroom.``
"Sure Cali they just pulled in``. Its 8 oclock", I can hear the elevator
door opening standing there waiting for the door to open, waiting
for him to walk in. When he's away, I miss him so much. As the
door opens, I pucker my lips for him to kiss me. grabbing him and
pulling his shirt over his head guiding him to the bathroom to sit in
the chair taking off his shoes and socks as he sits there looking so
tired. Cali!!! "What did I do to deserve you"? "Baby time, me for you,
you for me. Baby water ready youll feel better after you bathe. Did
you enjoy Daddy?." 'That man aint 84 year old he was fishing like he
was in his twenties throwing that reel in pulling in them Croppies

and Perch". "I know he enjoyed himself. I'm glad you brought him here. Taking his shorts off getting in the tub, "what are you waiting for baby" ? "As I undressed, "how was the Spa " omg? They took good care of us babe I tryed to pay the bill they wouldnt let me they said paid in full. Baby i got money too. "My woman my wife dont pay for nothing I got you baby". we all came hom tired everyone is resting until dinner, Laying back on his chest water feels so good as he massages me," "Cali I can't keep my hands off you I couldnt imagine life without. I will never sleep without you ""oh, yes you will when I go on vacation with the girls ``. I'm really not hungry I could go straight to bed. "We have Family waiting for us. Turning to Raw baby I got so much to tell you but i'm so tired we can sleep in tommorrow. Washing his body as he washes mine we stand up to rinse off in the shower, I grab you something to slip on. Grabbing my all purpose dress and a pair of panties to slip on. I can hear Troy and Honey talking, come on baby, let's do this.

Troy is so sweet she loves Pdiddy and "he Loves her black Love for real". Walking out the room. Hey Sissy you good" "yes hungry" "your ass got the munchies. Hey Daddy hugging him, hey Mama, Family. Mrs Laura standing there waiting to catter to us Mrs Laura please take a seat. Raw I hope i'm not overstepping But, Mrs Laura going on vacation She will no longer Be working in the kitchen. I would like for Maria to take over. Miss Laura is retired now. I want her to enjoy life to the fullest. I want her to come with me to Cali. She deserves to be catered to " "Baby this is your Castle you are the Queen this is yours to do as you please, nothing you do are say would be out of order". "I have a thing for the elderly Mother that caters to us. I love to cater. to them now. So from now on, Madam Star. Miss Laura. Molly. When I travel, they'll travel with me. Those are my three mothers. With that being said, let's enjoy our Dinner

So, Honey, what's the plan? I know you guys, going back to Cali tomorrow, and I just wanted to let you know. That Mona Lisa and Jewels got into a big fight. and, Jewels hit Mona Lisa in the head with a wine bottle. What? What? What? Yes, Honey, calm down. I know before I Came on this vacation that we should have gotten her and Took her to Madam Star. But she's ok. She got 20, stitches in the back of her head and that bitch ass nigga Dirty Red knocked, Jewel front teeth out. Only because he wants Mona Lisa to be his bottom bitch. Ok, this is the plan that I have. Madam Star will be retiring. And all the girls, they can either go and work with big Big Rella. She is really good to Rick's girls. Or. We're going to open up shops and give everyone jobs.., I'm not sure yet, Raw. Those four lots you purchase. What do you wanna do with them, babe"? "Well, Cali, your call." Just get them up and running`. I was thinking we could open up. A Pecan Candy Shop. Arc a Daiquiri shop. A beauty shop. And a Hair Salon. Chee Chee wants to work. Chee chee never traveled, so we'll have her come out here and she can do nails. Precious, Princess. and Bre and my niece Hope and Chaney do hair and Lashes they are good at doing makeovers. Here or in Cali. Whoever you want to put in the shops Raw. Honey We still have to get our shit up and running. Let's enjoy dinner. Mama you ok you look a little pale, I kind of feel tired you need to rest? "Yes, I guess I'll turn in early, a long day tomorrow". I'll help you no, baby i'm fine, i'll help you then", thanks Daddy. Goodnight Family. "Honey, we must tell her we know, waving her hand. I hate when she does that shit!" "Not now Cali", well when?" "I'm so aggravated, someone Bless the food, Lord thank you for the food we are about to eat purify it make it wholesome for the body Amen. Molly, you ok?". Yes, "Cali I don't understand what's going on. Are you leaving California"? No, Molly. I'm gonna be traveling back and forth. and as I said earlier, you, Madam star. And Mrs Laura will travel everywhere I travel. You guys or my mother's? You know how much I miss my mother. I even hate talking about this because it's so touching. I'll never get over That she is no longer here with me. Sometimes I can smell her in the room. That White Diamond that she loved so much. You'll never have to worry about a job, Molly. Come on, mommy. You are my everything. I will be getting married. Of course you know that. Molly, you'll be ok. Never worry about nothing. I got you, Mommy. Just so that everyone knows, Madam Star. Been keeping a secret. She is sick? She has Colon Cancer. I don't know how long, She has to live. She's so stubborn. She hasn't told no one. I hope she gets better. Because we don't know how long she has had Cancer or what the Dr told her. but when we get back to Cali, she'll go to the best doctor in the world". "Mija don't cry." "That Woman. Has been good to me. Raw i'm overwhelmed can we just turn in for the night pouring a glass of wine. I'll see you guys at breakfast. We will be dining at Houstons for Dinner. Daddy thank you how was she," "she's okay baby She said she was just tired baby dont worry God got her Dr Jesus", I'm just really tired". "I have so much on my mind. I want to be able to enjoy us one more day please.. And I love all of you guys.. I'll see you In the morning, Goodnight. Getting up to exit the dining area. Raw grabs my hand, he knows my emotions, Is running wild. Baby, It's so much we need to talk about. I just wanna keep it real with you. I want you to know everything about me. Since you came into my world, and me came into your world, We both have a lot of things going on. "Yes. This empire", "We will build.as we enter the room I start pulling my clothes off ready to get that third ward pound pound put down .need some good Relaxation. Climbing in the bed laying on my back, Opening my legs wide . saying come get it baby! get your pussy looking at him as he climbs in the bed, licking my lips, kissing my neck, sucking my breast driving me crazy, my flow gates open with pleasure, me moaning, groaning. make love too me Raw omg fuck me . Rolling me over as I get on my knees doggy style, climbing slowly to the top of the bed. I put an arch in my back, tilting my ass in the air all pussy. He enters my hot body screaming his name Raw Raw Raw baby ohhhh it's so good daddy fuck me baby ummmmm, harder harder. Raw im cumming him whispering "that's what i want you doing baby" thrusting harder, faster "Cali, Cali", "yes Raw baby, baby get it daddy it's yours throwing it back at him rotating it whining up he going crazy knees shaking .as he explodes in this good juicy wet wet" . "awwwwww baby i love your ass Cali you got that good good" "say my name then!!!' As we lay in the bed him breathing hard, "damn girl you about to give a nigga a heart attack baby when I say hold up stop." "Naw nigga no stopping. so relaxed my body so satisfycd I roll ovcr kissing Raw lips, baby this pussy belongs only to you. I'm so glad it's me you choose. Little sexy ass Cali Redbone. Baby I wanted a change, New beginning." "Cali You Captivate me everything about you. Your beauty and your booty". "Smiling baby, one of my Sisters from the Mansion was missing. No one saw her or heard from her in a couple of months. When I came down here. She was seen with this Pimp, named Dirty Red. A old pretty nigga with greeneyes. I ran into him he tryed to push up on me when I was at the Cat Meow" "What is the Cat Meow? A Club owned by Madam Cat. One of my Mother In the game. Raw, It's so much we need to talk about we got nothing but time getting out the bed to wash up. Baby Monalisa my little sister got hit in the head by this bitch named Jewel, this old sleakstack, Big Bird looking bitch, Dirty Reds bottom bitch she had to get stitches, When we get back we going in !!To get her back we can pay her debt or it can be some Gangster shit. "Cali;!!! "Baby no, I just did 38 years in Angola we are not doing shit. I got them boyz", "and I got them girls", lol Cali your ass is crazy. Let's get some rest or we can go another round lol". you can't handle me" shit i'll hose your little ass down. I got that A-1 Dick. don't I" ?? "Baby you the man rolling over hugging him." Raw, don't get out of this bed in the morning wake me up befor you shower ima need that again. I love you my King." "love you more Cali. sweet dreams my Queen. You know Cali I don't know how y'all do it in California I'll feed a motherfucker to the Gators down here "I know baby Dirty south". "Ya heard me?

Lol." "go to sleep". Rolling over thank you Lord for my Family Lord touch Madam Star, heal her body, Bless this man you gave me, my gift I adore him, teach me how to cater to him. closing my eyes sexually satisfyed, drifting off into LaLa land. Only God knows the plan for me. As I drift off I had a dream I ran into the D.A, I jumped, waking up ```"baby what's wrong"? I had a dream more like a nightmare. I must tell you something. I dated a D.A". "Cali Was he white" ?Yes, "how did you know?" "Just guessing". "He thinks he owns me baby" "Cali you're all mine, i'll fix any problem you have dont worry baby go to sleep. Come here you're safe with me wrapping his arms around. I'm sure he loves his family!!!!' "Lord, I lost my Mama last year, please heal madame star miracle working God tears roll down my eyes." "Cali you ok?" "Raw she's sick, I can't lose her baby". "We will go to the Holistic Dr. and get herbs we will cater to her. Phone beep, it's a text from Big Rella, "call me when you're free we can talk i'm here for you I know mama is sick Honey called me. "Congratulations on your engagement we can facetime in the morning I gotcha!!" "Did she just say I gotcha??? Hell naw thinking ok! I can't sleep. Ima take a bath, "i'll run you some water" no baby sleep. "Cali I got you baby". Walking into the bathroom, turning the light on dim baby it's already 3:20 am. As I get ready to play my gospel list. Raw plays my jam Deliver me we have so much in common we both or Sagittarius born in December. We know each other, we both have good Hearts, as my song comes on we both throw our hands up saying Hallelujah. Oh Lord I need you today Jesus i'm going threw so much, as tears roll down my eyes I drop to my knees. Weeping Praising God Thank you Lord Hallelujah "Praise him Cali" as Raw gets on his knees Holding me "Cali, while in prison I prayed, God send me someone to love and someone to love me and he sent you. Cali I got you. As we pray, Raw says Thank you Lord for better Dayz!!!You Lord hold the blueprint to me and Cali life. Tears rolling down his face. "Didn't think I would make it out but God said I'm going to give you a second chance at Love and Life. Baby I kept the faith. I thank God for you. He set me down to spare my Life in my younger days. I was moving too fast, Everyone forgot about me". "Raw no they didn't forget you, they just kept it moving. Kept Living their Lives". Lifting me up from praying God got us !!!"Never knew Love felt like this, never knew Love like this. I never dealt with a woman the long way "what's the long way babe"?(Loyalty). "but you, Cali Redbone you every real nigga Dream you changed the game", pouring oil into the bath turning on the jet stream water bubbling. "Cali you want a glass of wine?" "Sure baby, as he walks to the room, he gets two glasses you have a lighter "yes in the drawer'. As he pour the wine we look at each other the love we have for one another it feels so good. We toast to us Team Raw, for life my Queen " yes my King". Sipping on my wine is so refreshing. Raw steps into the tub reaching for my hand. Looking at our rings sparkling on the ceiling, he smiles with them gold teeth shining and me shaking my head, he says "what wrong?" "You're fine ass, "yes and I'm all yours". As I slip down in the tub putting my back against the jet pushing out a powerful stream on my back feels so good." "Cali, I'm glad Big

Mama knew it was you. She said son you must meet this gal from California named Cali Redbone. She is so beautiful inside and out. She is a daughter, in the game she is special, she is loving, "what! months ago what you waited" ", yes I was preparing for you, I didnt know that, had to get my shit in order. I knew I was done with the woman down here, they forgot about me when I was convicted, out of sight out of mind type of shit, "lol, they going to hog tie your ass and cut your balls off". "Laughing so hard shorty you crazy. Cali tomorrow I'm going to see a man about buying a private jet A Cessna citation xls 7 passenger" "wow". Im going to fly our family back to Cali and stop in Kansas City to drop pop off." "Wow, are you sure"? Yes, babe I'm sure we need to get them Lots up and running. Cali we need to keep the money coming in. I make a good Pecan Candy, that's how I survived in prison, me and diddy selling candy. Not to mention I had a few partners send me money who didnt forget about me. I got some stories to tell you. Laying back relaxing as I get up to sit by Raw sitting between his legs" "awww shit dont start nothing Cali, you can't finish" giving him a little lap dance, rotating on him bending over just a little bit as he guides it in me he grabs my hips. I slowly go up and down. "girl you don't even know what you do to me. If I would have known you before prison became my lot I would have put you up somewhere safe. As I get up, I turn around to look him in his face cause this man love I can feel it's real he touches my soul. sitting on him reaching for my joystick, its brick hard putting it in my juicy wet wet, slowly sitting down on it, omg baby you dont know what you do me either. Calling Raw name riding this dick up and down nice and slow as he sucks my breast driving me crazy licking his lip as he start caressing my breast taking his time licking my nipples sucking them driving me crazy as my flow gates open with ecstasy, riding that dick like i'm riding a wild bull up and down. Raw making sex faces grabbing his neck whispering in his ear daddy get this pussy, Here he goes" "wait Cali" "naw nigga its mine why i got to wait fuck me Raw get this pussy. what's my name say it say it Cali, Cali who? As I climb off that dick baby you good" "naw Cali im sprung" laughing you crazy let's shower give me a minute girl ok ima jump in the shower as i get ready to step in I bend over teasing Raw, mooning him nothing but pussy in his face lol he gets up I step in the shower lathering my rag running water over my body soaping my body he gets in an gets behind me pushing me over soap suds runs down my back to my ass damn girl bring that pretty ass here slapping my wet ass, and says" "all mine" "yes yours". Getting up to wash our bodies he gets the rag put on some bodywash smelling like strawberries he start washing my body from head to toe as I sit in the shower chair washing my breast then he start washing my treasure box slowly with a little force I open my legs as I moan he show, no hows to please me I moan with pleasure as my flow gates open satisfying me, I stand up he turns me around washing my back. Baby get you some rest i'm going to shower up and go workout, and have coffee with pops, he said he gets up at at 5am to pray and, read his bible every morning im going to have bible study with him. Cali I love God first then you yes in that order, reaching for the towel I turn to him kissing his lips. Wake me up at 9. Tell Diddy if Troy wants to come over before we leave. Love you babe walking to the bed I drop my towel and climb in on his side grabbing his pillow it smells just like him. Closing my eyes a vision of Mama comes to me "Cali he is the one baby you will live a good life with him he is the one baby. This man cherishes you" as she fades away mama, dont leave. I miss you so much. I just need to hold you and kiss you please don't go. Tears rolling down my face "Cali you call me" "no baby. "Are you good? Yes, Sleep my queen". Hour later I hear a knock at the door. Honey comes in "Cali mama getting weaker I see it in her face", "stop it!" "Cali you dont hear me. Mamas tired" "dont say that we gotta get her to a treatment center. Raw is buying a jet today. We are going to fly our family home", "A Jet shit I'm going to pilot school" "the hell you aint your ass smoke too much weed". "Sistah im happy for you dont worry about the D.A ill kill his old cracker ass myself" "this man loves you I heard him praying crying out to God, thanking god for his family his wife and children lol yell heffa kids, shit I see three lil Raws in your future running around. "Oh by the way, Big Rella texted me she said you called her, yes I was thinking mama could stay with you and Molly and Mrs Laura could help out they love mama, while we handle our business". "I'll set up an appointment with the Realtor for the two buildings, the one on Crenshaw and the one on Vermont. So Friday we can meet up with him. the wedding will be planned after we get shit going, I refused to shack up i'm wifey. I got to come back here and get stuff in order, I figured we can go to Houston's on saint Charles tonight and if everything go well Raw gets the plane we can leave in the next two days. Sis how's Ed"?. "He's good. He said I need to sit still. I'm always on the go, true". "Chasing that bag if it doesn't make dollars, it doesn't make sense". "Ok ima talk with Big Rella and see what's going on how many girls Mama have" "I think 8" "wow "Ok we can open up shops they all can have jobs and be part of Team Raw ". "Hell naw they will still us blind. They can just go with Big Rella". Ok I got to talk to Madame. I hope she agrees to everything. You know I thank God for Raw" "Cali listen, I dont want you to fear or worry about the D.A ill invite him over mama house. Tell him you're in the basement and knock his ass down the stairs". "Your ass is crazy, I'm not worried about him. Raw knows all about him" "ok give me a hug I love you sis", "ok let me get up. I'll be down in a minute, I need to freshen up" "ok see you downstairs Cali ". "As I get up walking to the dresser to get something to slip on, the phone rings its big Princess hey girl" "hey Cali, Mona is good she is still in Hospital she asked for your number I gave it to her. I know I should've asked first", "No you good babygirl, she's my little sister". "She should be calling you soon. She said she wants to get away from Dirty Red, but she owes him money". "Did she say how much"? "no but she's getting discharged tomorrow. I can get her and put her up somewhere til you get back, she's on coke. She asked me if I could get her. He got her strung out. "I'll get her in rehab dont worry, let me see where her mind is once I talk to her. Baby what's your cash app ima send you some money". "Thank you Cali, it's The Princess $. It's a picture of Jap. Ok got you i'll be back Friday night i'll see you Saturday do me a favor tell lil Princess and Precious, Chee Chee and Heaven and Bre we need to have a meeting saturday at the Cat Meow Club at 7 pm" "Ok Cali I gotcha omg stop using that word please" "you hate that word, why?. Please tell me ``"someone who was supposed to love me said I gotcha and that's what they did to me. Ok i'll send that to you see you soon". Let me slip on some clothes family downstairs, I grab some jeans and Tshirt as I walk in the bathroom to brush my teeth its a gold box from the jeweler smh I walk over to the sink pick up the box, opening it wow a beautiful ring with Baguettes Diamonds in in it at least 30 something Diamonds 1 2 3 4 5 6 10 20 30 31 32 33 34 35 36 37 38, Awwww represents time 38 years love this man as I slip it on my finger. I read the note it said, ``Cali, I waited 38 years to be free to find you. It was worth the wait. I used to ask God why? Everyone was getting out but me. Now I know why I was waiting for you to come into my life. I love you Cali Redbone...... What a beautiful sparkling gift. I love you Raw as I brush my teeth. Oh shit I almost forgot let me send Princess this money.$300.00. Looking in the mirror. Thank you for my Deliverance. On my way out the room I open the door there he is, looking him in the eyes baby, thank you so much for loving me, thank you for gifting me this special ring representing time i'll forever treasure it. "Cali that wasn't for you laughing, no other women deserve this but you baby". "I was about to slit your throat. Everything good", "yes. Prayer with Pops was amazing" ``. He prayed for Madam Star he said Dr Jesus will fix it. !!!! Give me some suga "you no I can't touch you without wanting you". Ok let's go have breakfast after you let me kiss them lips. As I walk out the room phone beep, its Chaney Cali my Parole Officer said if I have somewhere to go I can leave the halfway house in one week, Ok, you good see you Saturday. Texting her back. You're my sister for life. We can fix any situation you have. Walking down the stairs Good Morning Family, "hey hun" hey Daddy. Honey on phone good morning Eddie, yelling in the background, she's in good hands.

"Where's Mama? "She's out by the pool, she said she needs some Vitamin D". "Hey Mrs Laura and Molly" "bueno dias mija". "Daddy how you feel? "Oh my stomach is bothering me a little bit but im ok baby". "You have to get that checked out. You've been saying that for a minute".i'm going to check on mama walking down the hall. I hear God say the Blessing of the Lord maketh rich adds no sorrow. Yes Lord, thank you. Walking out to the patio she's relaxing with her shades on laying on the chair with her Ice Tea. Morning mama, how's my special lady "Cali I feel better today. Thank you for loving me, baby Mama Bird would be so proud of you". "I miss her so much tears roll down my eyes" "come here" "reaching her loving arms around me. I just melted", "baby I'm sick Cali I've not been honest to your girls. I have Colon Cancer ``"mama we know, we were just waiting on you to tell us", How do you know?. "We all know you're going to be alright". "No Cali the Dr gave me six months" Yes to get better!

As Daddy says Dr Jesus got you. Lets get you in. It's breakfast time and the family is waiting for you. I love you mama. I love you more. She looks at me, Cali I know Raw is the man for you smiling. As we walk in the door all, eyes on us. Morning, Mama Honey says. Daddy gets up and pulls out her chair. Raw pulls my chair out and we all sit there as food is being served. Maria is now in control of the kitchen. Mrs Queen Laura is seated. I look at her and smile. As we sit there a moment of silence everyone looks at me, "Cali you ok, yes why sis"? Today is the day Mama Bird got her wings, Omg I forgot to busy being sad, Daddy says "she is with king Jesus", my emotions kick in as I get ready to push away from the table. Raw "says no, baby you not running take a deep breath", "breath she here with us, Honey says, I was in my room and out of nowhere, I smelled white Diamond, Thank you family as I grip my Urn necklace on my neck holding it tight. "Daddy comes over and say I love you Sunshine". Daddy blesses the food as we bow our heads, Lord thank you for another day. We thank you for each other. We thank you for what you are doing in our lives. We thank you for the food, bless the hands that prepared it and bless my Cali on today Amen... Yes, green tomatoes grits over easy eggs smothered potatoes toast bacon ham or turkey chop. Great job Maria, no Cali Mr Raw cooked omg honey your the best, yes "I am for my Queen, tomatoes out the garden fresh pick just for you". Honey says "Raw thank you for loving my sister, she's so happy". "Tonight we will be dining at Houstons. And in two days we will be flying in our family jet Raw just purchased." "what ?????" "Congratulations Son", "yes pop you should hang out with me today so we can go check it out sounds like a plan". "Who will be flying it? "Honey says me. I was just looking on google's how to fly a Jet" "the hell you aint Daddy says. Lord forgive me she smokes too much of that weed". "I hired a Pilot named Jimmy who has been flying for

30 years' '. "Enough talking let's enjoy breakfast". "Pop we will drop you off in Kansas, and a driver will pick you up". "Wonderful I miss being home I made an appointment at the V.A." "As I look over at Raw, babe you not eating"?, "No, I had coffee and a Banana muffin. I'm good, I'm going down stairs to workout a bit" "Finishing my breakfast, I love fried green tomatoes, Raw stops and says "when Diddy comes tell him i'm in the basement". Phone ringing its Big Rella. "Hello Cali, how's Madam? here she is, hello Queen how are you doing``?''fine honey child how's Rick/fresh? tell Pretty Ricky I miss his money and when I get back I'll be talking with the D.A, he owes me A Favor". "Looking confused", "yes Cali the D.A is on the case" smh looking at Honey she rolls her eyes at me. "Baby dont worry I'll cut his throat myself" "Mama dont talk like that. Or I'll stick him with my ice pick. As Daddy looks around he gets up shaking his head" "i'm going to watch tv, you ladies or crazy. See you at dinner". So "Rella says what's the plan with the girls I havent talked to Mama yet". "We will be back to see you on Saturday ", "ok kool. We can link up at Madamn Kat. She's having a Birthday party for her son Ted. He's turning 50, ok talk to her i'll be on standby yall have a good day." "Thinking to myself Rella does good with Rick girls, they are some bad Bitches top shelf all different Nationalities. I havent seen Mama girls yet but, keeping it real I would rather give them jobs. But young girls like that fast money. "Honey what are we going to do? Thinking, We got alot going on. Sometimes I wonder why it's not enough time in the day". "Well Mac bomb called me and said he'll lead the girls and he'll move into the Mansion and guide the girls under mama instruction". "Chaney needs our help and Monalisa needs a program but let's purchase the buildings and get them up and running. Also daddy has been going to the Dr. Lately I need to check on him. He promised he would tell me if something was

wrong with him but I just feel like he isnt keeping something from me. "Focus sis". I lose my thoughts sometimes. I need to get back to Church. I had so much peace when I was in church. If you see me in deep thought I'm stressing "God got you Honey says whatever you're praying about god got you". Raw came into my life. He makes me feel complete, he touches my soul and he got that A1. Ok I need to go talk to my baby i'll see everyone in a minute let Maria no after breakfast she can have the rest of the day off. Walking down the hallway to the elevator I hear a voice say you can do all things through Christ Jesus that strengthen you. That's a scripture that stuck with me. Walking in the Elevator pushing the button to the basement. I walk out Raw is on the treadmill Hey babe, kissing his lips you good no I need a hug. As he stopped the treadmill what's wrong nothing just got alot going on. 'Cali I got you I can get you some assistant". "No babe, I'm good. Mama, Daddy, Monalisa i'm overwhelmed "youll be ok.

*

You just need some rest. youve been on the move since you've been here. We need a vacation just the two ""I have meetings and alot going on. We can do that babe, make love, swim, eat and watch movies. Sounds like a plan." "Shorty I will be up in like 30 minutes so we can rest or go swimming then start getting ready. See you up stairs, love you Raw. Walking in the elevator door closed all of sudden I smell white Diamond Mama you came I miss you so much, as I reach the top floor I smell the scent right infront of me. As if she is standing infront of me or walking past. The door opens and I look back and step out suddenly and the door closes. I turn, Daddy is there hey hun something wrong no dad i'm good. I Start to tell him what happened then when I open my mouth something esle comes out my mouth. Dad, we are going out to dinner this evening.

I'm going to the pool. It's therapy for me. "I'm going to get coffee and check on madam star" "ok love you dad. As I Turn walking I look back and daddy is looking at me with this strange look like he wants to say something to me. Walking out my phone ring it's an unknown number. I answered, "Cali, Cali, please help me, Mona. What's wrong babygirl "I need to get away from Dirty Red, he keeps me on dope working for him. He said I owe him $20.000 for what? if I want to leave him. Where are you in the waiting room, "why didnt you call Princess' ' she on her way, I hope. He visited me yesterday and took my phone and read my text. "ok go to the basement lock yourself in the men bathroom and wait for Jv, and Princess to get you they will put you in a room til I get there yall be safe if you leave i'm not going to help you. I got too much going on. "Cali I'm scared he said he'll kill me". "Not before we get his ass bitch, snap out of it let me call Jv stay put. As I stroll down my phone about to call Jv. I got a text from Mona phone saying, you dont want to play with me Cali Redbone! Calling Jv go to the hospital Monalisa in the basement the men's restroom gear up. pass her to Princess and terminate Dirty Red if you see him. Cedar Hospital. Scout the parking lot out first, get her and call me". "Ok Cali. Texting mona phone you want to live nigga dont you ever text me ill kill you and, your Bloodline on my Mama Bitch boy Ya Herd Me. Getting ready to change into my bathing suit, asking God to forgive me Lord let this go smooth as I change I hear the elevator door open in the basement Raw must be done hurrying up grabbing my towel, slipping on my sandals if, Raw see me it won't be no swimming as the elevator door open I open the room door and slip out. Tipping out the side door I can hear Daddy praying. As I walk out honey ass out here laying out in a chair sipping on wine.

"Girl you took so long." I set my phone and towel down. We have a problem.! Dirty Red that aint no problem I got him no I put Jv and Vell on his ass. Walking to the diving board to jump in I bounce twice and dive in. The water is so refreshing. I swim to the other side touching the wall turning around swimming to the deep side. This is what I needed for some cardio. As I come up I hear my phone ring. It's the Realtor missed call. Calling Bob back' I missed your call I just wanted to let you know Cali they accepted the cash deal ""Wow Hallelujah Thank you Jesus". "I sent you the information Via email. You can wire the money directly to them. And the building is all yours and Honeys. I'll get the keys and paperwork". "Thank you Bob". "No thank you, me and my family will be on Vacation, "ok i'll be in town on Saturday," "ok i'll leave paperwork at the frontdesk". "Honey we got it the building is ours" "Honey screaming which one? on Crenshaw they took the offer. We got it baby, baby that building takes up half of the block. We can open up four stores in the building God you're so good. Let's get ready for dinner. We got to celebrate. Ok i'll see you in a bit. Walkin in, what's all that screaming about we will tell you at dinner. Family, let's get ready for dinner. Walking to the elevator I can hear Raw talking on the phone. I walk to the shower and drop my bathing suit. All I hear is son ima get back with you, I turn and laugh. I know how to get his attention. I know how to get his attention, laughing babe I just wanted to tell you daddy wanted you oh ok you owe me yes pussy on the platter! Walking towards the door everyone is getting ready for dinner. babe hurry back ima take a quick shower as he walk out i start thanking god for the property we know own me and Honey. Lord help me not to procrastinate help me take care of business I got alot going on Lord you know all about it as I get out the shower I hear a voice say Cali watch out for wolves in sheep's clothing ok lord getting ready i'll just slip on something comfortable .my phone ring its my childhood friend, collect call from Spider. Hey, what's going on? I haven't heard from you for a long time. Are you good? Yeah. well I'm down here in New Orleans. You know, The Dirty South,. I'm down here with Honey and Madam Star and my dad. I talked to Flood and he asked about you.. do you need anything? wait!! hold up forgive me, you in prison ima send you some money when we get off the phone dont ever hesitate if you need something thank you cali some niggas dont even have shit up in this place when you go too jail people forget about you .well you know what they say out of sight out of mind even family forget you i guess they think three hots and a cot you good. I got you. So what's going on with your case? Have you Appealed, or filed some motions. I got your email.. You said you got the book." "Yeah cali it's a good book some of my homies order it too I'm proud of you". "I've been working on part two of the book. I got a lot going on. Here. Yeah. When I get back to Cali, I'm opening up a beauty supply and a beauty shop. I've got the building I told you about me and honey. So we're gonna make it do what it do, but in the meantime. And in between time. If you need anything, all you gotta do is Holler Remember. I'm just a phone call away. You my Brother for life. Ok, "take care and I'll talk to you soon". Alright, love you. "As I prepare to get dressed. It's getting late. I need to. Just get away. Get to myself. To be quiet, to hear when God is speaking to me. I need your guidance. Lord, I need your directions. I need for you to order my steps. Lord only You know what I need to do concerning these properties concerning the business concerning Monalisa and Chaney the whole crew help me, Lord touch like never before, let me find the right doctor for Madam. Raw enters the room,". Baby Honey and Pops works well with Madam. They should be together. Who, madam, star and pops that wouldn't work? Daddy likes younger women, his wife died of cancer. He just loves people. He knows how much I love Madamn.

star. Shower so we can get out of here. I want us to drive. It's been a minute since we drove somewhere. I can blow your socks off while you drive. "He'll naw Cali you might make me wreck you know you got that good good that drive a nigga crazy. You aint like no woman I ever had. when I went to prison they all moved on to the next nigga thinking I would never get my freedom I told myself loyalty, bitches dont know what that mean. but when I was in the streets bitches was my least worries you and me against the world Cali. "God made you just for me." "We can have Diddy drive the family. I just need some time." "Ok babe you need this A1". "I just need to be in your space. Ok i'll see you downstairs are we dressing up no babe casual. Ok love you see you downstairs. As I turn to get something out the closet Raw walks in the bathroom to shower, I grab my white Linen suit slipping it on putting my hair into a ponytailb grabbing some loafers and my purse, I'm leaving out babe. Ok beautiful. Walking out the room forgetting my phone on the charger walk back in Raw is praying as I stand there he says Lord teach me how to love Cali like no other man has. Wow this man here thank you Lord is all I can say. Walking out I see my Dad and Honey walking towards the den. Hello family everyone read" ?YES. "I'm starving". "Once Raw comes down we can leave. Diddy will be driving the family and me and Raw will meet you guys there. "Ok Kool where's Madame" she coming, she went to the restroom. Daddy says baby I took a nap could eat a horse, but when i look at him he turns away something aint right. We will be leaving and we need to be all packed Saturday we will be leaving, Raw walks down the stairs, looking so fine my panties get wet just thinking what he does to me. As he walks up I smell the same scent he had on when I first came here. It's like ive been hypnotized, He looks at me and I shake my head he knows what that mean, he walks over and whisper all this chocolate belongs to you shorty, lol i could eat him alive. Family Diddy is waiting outside. ill see you there where Mrs Laura ? "Here I am Cali, I was writing a list for the kitchen". We only got two days and Maria needs to stalk the kitchen". How's Diamond? She's fine, please tell her I need to see her before we leave, Daddy you looking good Houstons here we come, Team Raw. Walking to the Black Bentley Raw walks over, opens my door and says can't wait to get back home, me smiling cause I know what that means. Reaching for my hand girl I love you so much kissing my cheeks, getting into the car. Raw walks to his side and gets in, we look at each other and at the same time we both say thank you Lord. Oh Cali you want to drive yell but not this car you know what i want to drive as i terk a little bit he just smiles. Houstons on Saint Charles. As he pulls off, I recline my seat to relax. You OK baby yes, You know, tomorrow we need to meet at the construction site. construction site. See what's going on? They start building on two of the lots. Wow, baby, you ain't playing, baby. You told me to get shit going and I did just what I was ordered to do. You know, I got a lot of shit going on in Cali when I get back. I gotta get shit in order there too. Me and Honey got some stuff we need to make it do what it do. Because. As he plays my jam, Lover and friend, smiling at me. Lord this man you gave me, I'm grateful to be called his woman. He is every real bitch dream come true dream come true, He is a beast in the bedroom. He's loving, kind. and, he loves God. all A1. I get a text from JV. We got Mona, Lisa Kelly. She's good. I'll bring her to you on Sunday. Okay, JV, thank you. If you need anything, just give me a call. Did you see Dirty Red? No, I threw Mona Lisas phone away so that he couldn't track her. I left it in the man's bathroom down in the basement. Baby Daddy is keeping something from me. I feel it. November the 18 is his 85th birthday. I brought two houses down in Kansas City, fixer Upper and I had them remodeled. Daddy was in charge of everything. He doesn't know I bought those houses for him so he could have extra money. Also, I'm gonna buy him a brand new truck because he drives an old run down truck right now. Kelly Pops would tell you baby if he was sick, I think. When you talk to him, does he talk or say anything? No baby, we only talk about the Lord. The freeway crowded it's friday baby the saints having a game tommorow. Are you going? Naw I got something planned for me and you ok!!! remember we got to go to the site to see What's the progress, oh yell that's right we got to pack up. We are leaving out Sunday morning right? Yell baby. as we cruise Canal st. it seems like all eyes on us, A red benz pull up hey, "Hey Raw how are you doing? you aint returned none of my calls" Raw looks over at me. I rise up from my reclined seat and she looks surprised, hey!!! "I Lay back down", "oh who is she"? "my wife Cali Redbone" "that's why you aint returning calls" "I laid back knowing Raw got this never let a bitch see my sweat or bring me out of character. Cause one thing for sure our love can't be broken we both know what loyalty is.as she pulls off she jumps in front of us and stops on breaks. Bitch aint knowing if I was in Cali and she pulled some shit like this. I air her tires out. She acts like she wants us to hit her car. Raw steps on brakes I look at him and blow him a kiss baby our shit on lock. I'm prepared for your run ins cuz I no you got it under control i'm a lady at all time my presence makes a bitch shake. They regret they left you to die in Angola. Besides beauty is to be seen not heard that's what mama used to say". "you crazy Cali ya heard me"!.as we turn off the bright lights up it's N.O.PD in the mirror damn babe you got your strap on you "naw its put up" ok. Tonight ain't the night. approaching the car a black officer walks up "good evening you made a turn without signaling I almost ran into you". Looking over The officer looks and says Ron

Wiggins Raw turns, "awww man what's good reaching to open the door to step out. It's gots to be someone he grew up with from the magnolia projects.as they talk, the Officers walks to the car and says "sorry for pulling you guys over, Cali Redbone! I read your book. My wife couldn't put it down, she was laughing and crying and never knew I would run into you down here. Ain't you from Cali, yes you can sign my book next time I see you guys ""sure!!! Book 2 coming soon "" wow can't wait to read it. hope this doesnt ruin your night". I look and turn my head. Raw gets back in the car baby we used to hustle back in the game shit he must've not read your license plates we pull off heading to our destination. Driving a few blocks pulling in. The Family is already there. The Valet opens our door as we step out. Raw reaches for my hand, kisses it and we walk in and a Server comes up right t. Honey crazy ass said what took you long ?Traffic!!!!. Raw pulls out my chair sit down look over to my left Daddy looks at me and turns his head it looks like something is bothering him, waiter walk up my name is Paula im you waiter for this evening, let's get you guys started with drinks please, as I raise my hand i'll have a blended strawberry Margarita make that two. Honey says with two shots of patron. Raw what you want baby Hennesy on rocks. Dad ginger ale mama coke Mrs Laura pepsi. Diddy patron on rocks. Molly kahlua and milk plz and glasses of water with lemon ok i'll be back with rolls and drinks here, Sitting in a beautiful secluded area dim lights thinking wow a change came for real all my loved ones here with us. Looking at the family realizing I'm so blessed thinking this man really brought my family here to be with us on our engagement. I'm not that hungry im going to have the Ruby Red Trout and coleslaw, baby what you having, looking at Raw i'll have some Cali Redbone hey now daddy says its kids at the table me and Mrs Laura, as we all laugh baby you eat that 1 all the time.

Rotisserie chicken baked potato broccoli and you dad I'll have the same as my son, *a great choice pops. Ok, here's your rolls, drinks and you guys are ready to order yes. yes 1 order red trout 4 order Rotisserie chicken. Diddy what you having burger and frys. Molly i'm going to have the scottish salmon. Honey says they aint got what I want girl just order. Her ass is always picky. I'll have the prime center cut mediumn baked potato, cesar salad oh some green beans we have broccoli, I want green beans ok i'll see smh she done smoked some that top shelf. As we sit here waiting on our meal sipping on my Margarita it's so good so refreshing picking up my shot of Patron daddy says hold on Cali ima have to carry you out. No daddy I'm good.ok babygirl mama you ok yes tired did you rest yes but aint no place like home. I'm worried about Monalisa she's good mama youll see her when we get back. So family we got two days we leaving everyone can start packing tomorrow i have some things to do in the morning so we won't have breakfast. Me and Raw got a early appointment (daddy) says you pregant im finally going to get my grandbaby, No Daddy Raw says that would be nice, stop it... you going to get them grandbabies we got to get everything in order first. as the Waiter brings our food Trout right here. The 4 rotisserie chicken goes right there all in a row. Thank you dishes or hot be careful. Prime center here. I hope you got my green beans. Yes, we do ok. And Scottish Salmon here burger right here Diddy says. salad here Honey reaches for it. Thank you A1 sauce lemons plz thank you miss Paula. Let me get that as she walks to Raw sir your family's meal has been paid for by a gentleman who is dining in the Vip. and says that's a beautiful family. I got there tab where is he right over there ok as Raw gets up, to walk over it's a Lawyer he had dealing with I rather not say his name as he approach him "hey man im glad your home beautiful family wish i had a family but no one believed in me so I decided to turn that page in my life and never look back, beautiful woman yes she's my gift from God, you didnt have to pay my bill I wanted too when I looked over and seen you my heart was filled with joy here take my card call me, if you ever need me by the way do you stll have Darryl number I got a job for him he really tried hard to get you out. Take care, remember family first and never trade her in for nothing or no one. Thanks man enjoy call me soon. will do. Raw comes back to the table, wow god is amazing "baby your food is cold, you want a new plate?" "naw im good". "Pops, how's your food"? "It's delicious" "that man who paid the bill is a Lawyer. When I was in Angola, he tried to work on my case but he didnt have the pull 25 yrs ago but, now he's one of the Top Dog Lawyers in Jefferson parish". The waiter approaches, will you guys like dessert? I'm stuffed. It was good 'molly you good yes mija". Ok any take out no we came to eat. Lol digging in my purse I get out a tip no maam i was tipped already. You got kids? give it to the oldest tell them it's from Cali Red, omg hold on as she walks away she come back with my book omg please, can you Autograph my book I love it I can't sit it down, is there a second part" yes, coming out in september, all my friend order the book I love your hair. please tell me how to get that color here, take my card sweety call me tomorrow. I got you signing the book. Love Cali Redbone. Here you go. Thank you so much my friends aint going to believe me well let's take a picture thank you so much. Family, you ready getting up everyone so tired i'll see you at home``. Standing up so full "Raw says baby i'll work it off you". walking to the car as valet parking pulls up we get in. Raw says baby we got so much to be grateful for first God then each other. "Baby take the freeway so we dont have any more run-ins". "Lol Cali you're crazy. ya heard me baby I wish my Ma could have met you she would have loved you". "I'm so tired we got alot going on as he reaches over and grabs my hand, nothing but death shall seperate us. And I pray we will be in our 100s when its our time. Baby if I go before you bring me back here and make sure I have a Traditional Funeral a second line ok baby whatever your heart desire. "You know Raw, I'm glad I came on this date with you, madam star just knew it was you for me, and me for you.. Have you ever met her before" No not until now? I just heard of her. Big mama was sitting at the table one day and said Raw, you need you a wife. I told her no i gotta get me right, for that special someone she said son, your wife aint from here, your wife is in another State I looked, she said yes son, she said by the way God is molding her just for you, I want you to meet someone she's always been special to me her name is Cali Redbone beautiful girl she lives out in cali she's single no kids, got her own shit not like theses woman after you for your money boy listen to me. Remember one thing: life has no Guaratees . matter of fact I'm going to call her right now and I said naw ma, some other time im dealing with someone." "Baby leave that gal alone. She aint the one dont waste your time son. Cali you will love, you just watch, we never spoke about you again, and that was a couple of months ago. and that woman that pulled up on us on canal street that was who I was dealing with. I wasnt into her, just somebody I was dealing with and, what about the broad at the Jewerly store she was thirsty, that's all I quenched her thirst a bit. she was too into me. I wasnt feeling her. So you brought them gifts too. No Cali, just you baby. . Babe one night I was praying. I asked God, Lord what is it I need to do to complete me and as I was praying the Lord said Cali is a gift from me to you, I told myself okay Lord, your will be done. The Bible says when a man finds a wife he finds a good thing. I looked at life differently from that day forward. I just stopped answering calls from her. I went on a fast praying asking God to change my heart so I can deal with Cali the long way I never dealt with a woman the long way baby, what's the long way? loyalty to you and only you. Before prison became my Lot I had dealings with quite a few women. Did you ever love them? No, I cared about one, what happened that she didnt stay down with you. She moved on, it's all about you Cali Redbone. The next day I went back to mama and said yes cali is the one for me God told me. Mama, call her, do whatever it takes to get her to visit me please!l, ok Son. whatever she did you're here and God allowed us to be. That very first time I laid eyes on you it was love at first sight your every real nigga dream Cali. awww you prayed for me yes I prayed to love you the right way you never have to worry about A women in New Orleans they dont know what Loyalty means. I was a good Nigga I looked out for everybody but they, forgot about me .wow baby im glad I came we almost home, pulling up to our home family is getting out the van. I open my door. "Raw says Cali I dont need help doing my job baby", "what's that "?opening my Queen door, I closed the door he gets out walks around opens my door thank you baby. Hey family everyone, good?." "Yes full and sleepy, Madamn star you ok?" "yes, an overtired, child you know black people can't eat, like this and function goodnight baby". See everyone tomorrow one more day here and we are on our way to Cali. See everyone for dinner, got a few things to do in the Morning. "Ok Sunshine". "Love you Dad" "I hope I get me some grandkids before I get too old to enjoy them". Love you too dad smh that man. As we walk through the Garage to the Elevator I push the button, the door opens. As we make it halfway to the second floor he stops the elevator and starts kissing me pulling my shirt over my head caressing my breast sucking them driving me crazy. I grab him and unzip his pants kissing his neck. This man smells so good I think he put a spell on me. I drop his pants rubbing his big juicy hard dick drop to my knees and go crazy. See, I aim to please Raw. I know what he likes, and what he needs. I just love this man as he moans. My touch drives him crazy. Raw pushes the on button the bedroom door opens as he picks me up and lays me on the bed pulling my clothes off. My pussy is so wet ready for him to thrust into me with that A1 as he climbs on me I get to shaking cause I know it's about to go down. See Raw was blessed with all the right tools he knows how to please me as he enters my treasure box I scream he puts his hand over my mouth and says they are going to think i'm killing you. "You are". Honey knows if she hears me screaming I'm climbing the walls. I grab his hand and start sucking his fingers, moaning with esctasy fuck me raw rotating on that dick driving me crazy cause he for real got that good good. As he grabs my breast I get on top he's "like naw cali". "Naw nigga its my turn as I sit on it slowly up and down. Raw start making them sex faces I know he is about to explode wait Cali wait a minute I ride him fast like i'm on a bull lol get it daddy get it awwwww Cali yes baby it's me your cali redbone get it daddy he grabs me and holds me so tight i know he is in lala land right now breathing hard shaking i rotate on that dick driving him crazy he grabs me stop cali wait i wind it up on him laughing you good babe yes no woman ever do me like you do me cali me smiling. I roll over he catches his breath and say come on round two i damn near run out the bed raw say you cant handle me cali nigga please i thought you was going to have a heart attack walking into the bathroom to used the toilet it just pours out of me like a water flow I sit there for a moment, this man here is every real bitch Dream.., lets bath ok let me catch my breath i bend over to put the stopper in before i know it raw is up behind me stop playing you know you dont want it we laugh as he kisses my neck wife i love you let bath and get some rest while waiting for the bath to run i brush my teeth Raw sits in tub washing his body he's tired and over satisfied Cali you dont know what you do me yes i do.. Raw gets up steps into the shower and I climb in the bath. see i know when he is tired he didnt wait for me to bathe with him lol . cali i'm going to sleep no you aint i want round 2 lol. Ok baby, I love you raw. as he steps out the shower to the sink to brush his teeth all that chocolate for me. I lay back thinking about what a busy day we have tomorrow. God thank you for all the women that have been in Raw's life. I salute them. But, this man here is all mine and they just couldnt hold him down, even if they did leave his side they should have made sure he had a bar of soap to wash his ass and deordarant. I just want to give a shout out to them and say thank you for moving out the way for his queen. I just love this man. Come on cali get your ass out the tub. come to bed. Ok stepping into the shower to rinse off, grabbing my towel walk past the mirror and all I see is a glow I had to walk back it was like I saw a ghost lol its was just a glow of happiness from that A1 pound, pound he be putting down. Drying off too get in bed.as I walk in the room Raw is knocked out snoring I climb in bed to kiss him he open his eyes and say "Cali me for you, you for me". Holding me in his arm don't start nothing you can't finish. Closing my eyes drifting off so satisfied, I reach for my phone to put the alarm on for 7am. It's 11: 45 now. Goodnight world Silently Praying for Our Family. Alarm beeping. I just want to roll over and turn it off but I know we got a busy day. {Raise and Shine My King} It is time to handle our business walking to the bathroom to brush my teeth. Raw says babe im tired awww suga me too let's get shit going you said we gotta keep turning getting shit up and running. combing my hair into a bun, baby why you dont wear your watch I will today. Come on babe slipping on a sundress, it's a hot day. Raw got up and went into the bathroom, his phone rang and I grabbed it. Answer it "Hello" a voice says who is this? "You called this phone. "I'm lookin for Raw. He aint got no Secretary. Well he does now and a wife and a ride a die, oh! "Is this Cali Redbone"?. "Naw this is Mrs Raw". "Oh is it", "yes. So how can I direct your call"? "I'm not going anywhere. I'm always going to be in his life. He cheated on me with you". "Boo Boo, hold up!!!! He didnt cheat on you, you was someone he was dealing with, until his Queen came on the scene anyway have a nice day as I got ready to hang up" she said "watch your back bitch." "bitch!!!!.. "I'm from the show me state make me a promise never a threat" .ummmm as I hang up. "I close my eyes and say no weapon form against me shall prosper carry on…. Raw walks out "what's wrong"? "holding his phone, he looks, you good ?" "yes my king we good you just got a call from someone but it wasnt nothing important". "babe slip on some jean and Tshirt hot day Babe beignet and coffee on our way to the site please". "Anything for my Queen" ok, let me go see the family meet you downstairs my love, ok walking out the door to go downstairs Maria, stop me and say "Cali I wash Madam linen she needs to see a Dr", "why is that? "she had blood and stool on the sheets", omg thank you, "please dont tell her I told you" "I won't trying to pull myself together, Honey walks out the room hey sis you look like you seen a ghost, no i'm good can't tell her she cant hold stuff like this in. Where's everyone?" "Out by the Pool breakfast was served outside in the Garden so peaceful Cali mama is sick "naw you told me she was aight as you say. She will get the best treatment when we get back." "Love you sis we can talk later. Walking out to the gazebo in the Garden Mama Daddy and Mrs Laura Molly are all having Coffee, hey Family "hey baby" how was breakfast? "It was delious". Ok we are going out to see yall at dinner as Raw comes out, "Goodmorning Family, Mrs Laura can I speak with you?" "yes,

Son", walking to the house "I notice Mrs Laura has a limp, ok all see you guys later", Raw returns "babe you ready? Yes, walking out Mrs Laura walking, what's wrong with your leg? I hit my knee on my bed. It's just a little bruised sweety. ok take care of yourself see you later. Babe I want you to drive no, this your neck of the woods. Ok your Coffee and Beignet and, off to the site. Cali baby you put me too sleep I was snoring like a bear thats what that good good do to a nigga lol. jumping on the freeway to get to st charles street Raw gets a phone call someone and says we be there in 20 minutes, driving beautiful day baby. I'm a build you a house from the ground Cali here in New Orleans. Your determin to make us live here no, baby when we come down to Mardi Gras and you have to take care of our property here. Ok I got shit going on in Cali baby we going to be traveling ive been down 38 yrs im not going to sit still. We are going to get everything up running then we are going on Vacation just us Baby, Mama is sick and I think daddy is too. I need some one-on-one time with him. I really need to know if he is okay. When my Mom died, I was so broken I had to pick myself up. I miss her so much baby I know the feeling. when my Ma passed I was in Angola she told me wasnt nobody going to Love me, are see about me like she would. She was right, hey babe I got a few partnas still down I need you to jpay them when you get back, I want to make sure they straight see my loyalty is real. Pulling up to saint charles I see Diamond standing out with our coffee, and that white bag can't wait to enjoy my coffee. "Hey babygirl." "Hey Cali Grandma told me you said come by before you leave. I wish I could go with you. If you like, I got to work. I need to talk to you. Please come by or call me if you still have my number. Yes I do. Ok see you later thank you. Raw, pulling off you got the hook up Mrs Laura text Dime and told her we were pulling up .omg I love this Coffee baby I promise to love you like no other, Cali why you Love me baby? God did this. Our Love was a gift from God. I needed you to complete me. Love is an action word and that's all you have been showing me, I feel it baby. So how's your son? He's good. Ok pulling up to the Site Tractors Digging men Hammering, wow they working do we need to take care of something no babe it's all good. That's Harvey, the head man in charge, all brothers working here in Cali. they all young Family Business Blacked Owned, they from Cali ofcourse, damn they working hey, Mr Raw I'm HNIC is that the company name? No Boss !!!{Im the Head Nigga In Charge) awww man you got me. laughing, so how's everything going well? We got everything we needed. We should be finished in two to three weeks with these lots then we will go over to the next site. Ok we are going to Cali for a week.- Raw passes him his card if you need anything call me, sure nice to meet you. Walking back to the car Raw says damn Cali you got them from California? yes, Raw we grew up together his brother got killed his brother robbed a bank, and got away some fuck boy got jealous and told the feds, they came too get him had a shoot out they wasnt going to take him alive . after his brother death, he changed his life and started a family business some of them workers are young ladies under them hard hats you lying naw seriously baby I know I needed you big mama said it, yes I was true to the game but not true to a weman .till I met you. baby lets get something to eat. i'll have a hot sausage samich and a coke this early it's almost lunch time. Ok let's go to the French Quarters and grab some food kool. See i'm so tired let's eat and take me home I want to sleep. Ill put you straight to sleep naw nigga im going to sleep, matter of fact babe we can just go home im to tired too eat you sure yes babe im good till dinner. let me call Mrs Laura to tell her we will have fried fish salad and Fries cali before pops tell you i didnt catch not one fish diddy caught two pops caught 12.as i reach for my phone in my purse I notice I haves bands of money like $20 racks I look at Raw, why baby its for Pops and Molly, Madamn star and Honey give them $5.000 a piece just a little spending money thats all awww you so sweet.as I yawn so tired laying back . I just want to climb in bed and sleep. I need a whole day to sleep mind body and soul is tired I hope that cat aint tired, stop playing you going to fuck me to death, lol naw Cali ima fuck you, right and tight. Looking at him shaking my head. Babe, tomorrow we leave going to cali you ready baby ive been there back in the game I use to score, ive been to southcentral and the bay area but i'm ready we got to pack what time will we leave ? what time is the pilot going be there ?i'll get that straight tonight at dinner.im get you straight then i'm going to take care of some business naw nigga what kind of business im going with you. You can never get caught up in shit that might seperate us, Cali you crazy yes about you we going to take a nap I thought you was tired not no more looking at him crazy .pulling up to the house diddy open my door hey cali hey Raw I see you upstair as he laugh. Walking in the house hey family can I speak to everyone ladies seated at the table having tea where is my daddy he laying down ok well just wanted to give you this its from Raw no I can't, take that Molly says, take it im tired or ill leave it on the table! i'm going to rest we leaving in the morning walking up to go upstairs i back track swing by Daddys room he's laying in bed hey daddy you ok yes sunshine my stomach upset that's all .if something was wrong would you tell me ofcourse ok daddy I love you see you at dinner im going to rest love you baby. walking up the stairs putting my phone on silent every time i go to rest, someone calls me. walking into the room smells so fresh Mrs Laura always make sure we are good, closing the drapes looking out the window I see Diddy and Raw and a nigga I never seen before.

Shit i'm tired as hell let me see what's going on walking to the elevator i hear someone getting on on the lower level waiting for it to come up it stops at 1st floor, As I walk to my door its Diamond coming to talk before we leave oh shit I forgot I told her to come by, opening the door hey Dime" ",Cali I didn't want you to leave without saying see you next time aww you so sweet". "I'll see you in the den ok". walking out the front door the team is there talking "hey babe you good "yes this my boy Aaron. "Nice to meet you. The pleasure is all mine Cali" "Raw im going to have a meeting with the Ladies ok, you not tired yell but, i'm going to have to handle this . As I turn to walk in daddy there hey daddy" hey baby you ok yes Cali", ok i'm going to have a meeting see you in a bit you need anything "no i'm good". walking in Dime and Molly Mama. Honey, Mrs Laura has a seat. Hey Family, we need to talk." "Honey says let me take notes", "she smoked some happy shit, ok first thing first we got alot going on business, jobs our Team is big we got shit to do money to make." ",Honey says can I get a roll call ok .

Team Raw[Honey Cali. Princess Precious Big Princess Bre Heaven, Deor, Jv, Monalisa, Mama Molly, Mrs Laura, Jaylin, Lavell Leon Josh Tank and Diamond Hopey Chaney and a few more the young people got jobs if they want to work, Me and Honey opening two shops in Los angeles and four here you can travel back and forth we will be leaving tomorrow was everyone able to get stuff in order? Well that's it let me know if any family members need a job first. We will be leaving in the morning everyone packed up? I'm going swimming. It relaxes me, anyone for a dip in the pool ?I'll meet you out there.. I'm going up to change"., Raw walks in the front door hey babe you good ?yes i'm going for a dip in the pool me and Honey, you lucky cause i'll come put it on you i'm going to make a few calls get the polit ready for our flight and pack i'll be waiting on you. ok, kissing him walking up the stairs. Hey Cali thank you for loving me I feel your Love. Raw nothing but death shall seperate us. As I walk in the room to put on my swimmingsuit, the phone rings. It's Princess, I'll call her later. Grabbing my towel out the linen closet walking pass the mirror I stop look in the mirror stairring in the mirror Cali watch out for the D.A he desire you still smh Lord please remove him keep him away from me give me warring Angels and Guardian Angels, mind start wondering I'll kill him help Lord i need you you gave me my soulmate and my pass is trying to haunt me Lord I need you to fix this situation. walking out the door, beautiful evening wind blowing fresh aroma of pine love it. the smell of Weed hit me that sister of mine sitting in a lounge chair smiling ear to ear crazy ass what took you so long talking to Raw setting my towel down i jump in swimming under water all the way across swoosh, feeling heart beating so refreshing as I come up Honey jumps in lol that sistah !!!! swimming back and forth body needed this .swimming to the other in getting out As I reach up Raw grabs my hand i step up and he jumps in with me lol this man as we drop to the bottom he kisses me underwater bubbles flowing up cause i'm so tickle we kick of the bottom as we shoot like a Rocket to the top surface as I swim away Raw right behind me I can hear Honey say i'm going in just what Raw wanted he grabs me closed to him kissing me i'm so ready I Melt in his arms throwing my legs around his waist pulling my swimsuit to the side omg he guides his brick hard dick in my super wet pussy I go crazy he walks me around pulling me up and down my moaning with ecstasy Raw ain't no joke as, I turn it's Daddy And Madam, I pushed away laughing at Raw glad I wasn't naked they sit at the edge of pool putting there feet in the pool beautiful night dad says i'm going to miss being with y'all we'll come with us to California dad no baby I got to go home, Daddy no one's at your house not even your dogs, I know baby it's been a great long two weeks awww thank you Dad for coming I had to come this man sent for me asked me could he marry you so I had too see him and make sure he is the one. Raw swimming doing Laps back and forth Ok Let me get out busy day tomorrow we finally leaving going back to Cali Can't wait so much is going on but I got this well, God got it. New Orleans been fun but it's that time to Make it do what it do Enjoy.

# DEDICATION

I dedicate this book to Mr. Raw Ron Anthony Wiggins. He encouraged me to write this book and stayed on me about writing the book. It's a story about love, change, second chance, God is going to open them doors and set him free! My son Pa Pa who said right the book Mama Briona & Diamond my two daughter kept asking me Mom you finish yet so here it is enjoy this book! And my sistah Pam Taplin who's an author already who said you got this! Nothing is too hard with God!

To my son Leon Smith and William Swan and Joshua Swan. I know you will enjoy this book, and by the time I finish my next book you'll be home.

Mama, I did it, I wrote the book!

Cali Red Bone

Coming soon book three.
Book three going back to CALI.

Printed in the United States
by Baker & Taylor Publisher Services